MATH ADVENTURES

GREG'S GARAGE SALE

A MONEY COUNTING ADVENTURE

by Elizabeth Everett
illustrated by Amy Zhing

GRASSHOPPER

Tools for Parents & Teachers

Grasshopper Books enhance imagination and introduce the earliest readers to fiction with fun storylines and illustrations. The easy-to-read text supports early reading experiences with repetitive sentence patterns and sight words.

Before Reading

- Discuss the cover illustration. What do readers see?
- Look at the picture glossary together. Discuss the words.

Read the Book

- Read the book to the child, or have him or her read independently.
- "Walk" through the book and look at the illustrations. Who is the main character? What is happening in the story?

After Reading

- Prompt the child to think more. Ask: Greg has a garage sale and adds and subtracts money. Have you ever counted money or counted back change?

Grasshopper Books are published by Jump!
5357 Penn Avenue South
Minneapolis, MN 55419
www.jumplibrary.com

Library of Congress Cataloging-in-Publication Data

Names: Everett, Elizabeth, author. | Zhing, Amy, illustrator.
Title: Greg's garage sale: a money counting adventure
by Elizabeth Everett; illustrated by Amy Zhing.
Description: Minneapolis, MN: Jump!, Inc., [2023]
Series: Math adventures
Includes index. | Audience: Ages 5–8
Identifiers: LCCN 2021058698 (print)
LCCN 2021058699 (ebook)
ISBN 9781636908649 (hardcover)
ISBN 9781636908656 (paperback)
ISBN 9781636908663 (ebook)
Subjects: LCSH: Counting—Juvenile literature.
Money—Juvenile literature.
Classification: LCC QA113 .E86 2023 (print)
LCC QA113 (ebook) | DDC 513.2/11—dc23/eng/20220126
LC record available at https://lccn.loc.gov/2021058698
LC ebook record available at https://lccn.loc.gov/2021058699

Editor: Jenna Gleisner
Direction and Layout: Molly Ballanger
Illustrator: Amy Zhing

Printed in the United States of America at
Corporate Graphics in North Mankato, Minnesota.

Table of Contents

Selling Toys

"Are you ready for our garage sale?" Greg's mom asks.

"Yes!" says Greg. "I'm going to sell these toys."

Greg puts stickers on the toys he will sell.

Small toys will cost one dollar each.

Big toys will cost ten dollars each.

$10
$1

“Here is thirty dollars to start with to make change,” his mom says. “Remember, you count the ten-dollar bills by tens. You count the one-dollar bills by ones.”

Greg adds the bills.

Greg's first customer buys six small toys.

"That will be six dollars, please," says Greg.

$1 + $1 + $1
$1 + $1 + $1
= $6
$1
$1
$1
$1
$1
$1
$10

He pays with a ten-dollar bill.

"You have to give him change," says Greg's mom.

"How do I know how much to give back?" asks Greg.

"Subtract the cost of the toys from how much he paid," his mom explains.

"So I give him four back!" says Greg.

He counts out four one-dollar bills.

"How much for this?" asks Greg's next customer.

"Ten dollars, please," says Greg.

She gives Greg a twenty-dollar bill.

Greg gives her a ten-dollar bill in change.

-10
20
10
$10
$20

Greg's next customer buys three big toys.

"Thirty dollars, please," says Greg.

"I only have a fifty-dollar bill," she says.

"No problem!" says Greg.

He gives her twenty dollars in change.

-10 -10 -10
50
20
$50
$20

Greg's last customers buy one big toy and two small toys.

They give Greg exactly twelve dollars.

"Thank you!" says Greg.

$10 + $1 + $1 = $12
$1
$1
$10
$1
$1

“How much money did you make today?” Greg’s mom asks.

“Fifty-eight dollars total!” says Greg. “I have enough money saved to buy a bike!”

$6+$10+$30+$12
= $58

Let's Review!

Greg imagines a number line. It helps him add and subtract numbers. Let's try it!

1. Using this number line, **add** the numbers to find the answer:

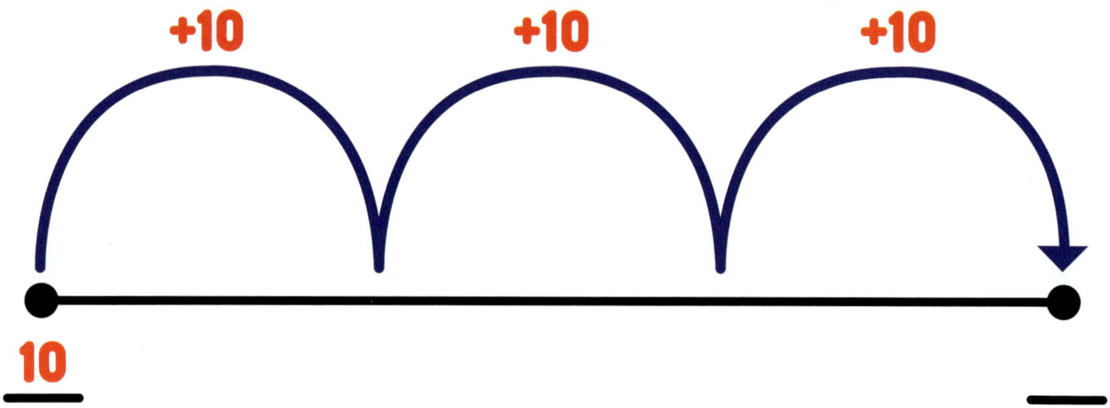

2. Using this number line, **subtract** the numbers to find the answer:

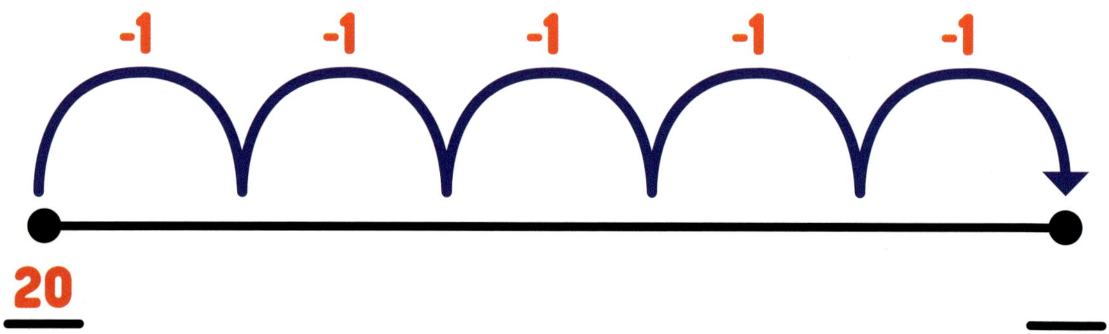

Let's Review! Answer Key: 1. 40 2. 15

Picture Glossary

bills
Pieces of paper money, such as a one-dollar bill.

change
The money you get back if you pay more than something costs.

customer
A person who buys things.

total
Making up the whole amount.

Index

To Learn More

FACT SURFER

Finding more information is as easy as 1, 2, 3.

1. Go to www.factsurfer.com
2. Enter "**Greg'sgaragesale**" into the search box.
3. Choose your book to see a list of websites.